For the children of East-The-Water Primary School, Bideford – P.B.
To my Santa, Eugene B. – A.C.

First published 2017 by Macmillan Children's Books
an imprint of Pan Macmillan
20 New Wharf Road, London N1 9RR
Associated companies throughout the world
www.panmacmillan.com

ISBN: 978-1-5098-3114-2

1 3 5 7 9 8 6 4 2

A CIP catalogue record for this book is
available from the British Library.

Printed in China

Santa Selfie

Peter Bently & Anna Chernyshova

MACMILLAN CHILDREN'S BOOKS

Santa was packing his holiday gear.

He chuckled, "I'm not doing Christmas this year.

The North Pole is freezing! It's not at all fun.

I'm not staying here. I'm off to the sun!"

"Just for one Christmas," he said to the elves,
"You'll have to deliver the presents yourselves.

North Pole

Rest of the World

Take care of the reindeer while I'm away.
I'll leave Little Elfie in charge of my sleigh."

Santa decided to start off his trip
By going for a sail on a luxury ship.
He waved as the sleigh flew away in the sky,
And called out to Elfie, "Merry Christmas! Bye-bye!"

"Ho-ho!" Santa smiled as he boarded the liner,
"A cruise in the sunshine! What could be finer?

Why do I stay in the Arctic? It's silly
Being stuck somewhere gloomy and lonesome and chilly."

Santa was sunbathing next to the pool,

Sipping a juice that was tasty and cool,

When a little boy's letter dropped out of his book.

A girl picked it up and had a quick look.

It said:

"Dear Santa, For Christmas I'd like
A new pair of football boots,
sweets and a bike".

"You're SANTA! That's AWESOME!" she gasped in delight.
"Can I take a quick photo?" Said Santa, "All right . . . "

CLICK!

"Thanks!" said the girl. "I must tell the others!"
And she ran off to fetch all her sisters and brothers.

"SANTA'S ABOARD!" Soon everyone knew,
Including the Captain and all of the crew.

Wherever he went, he heard people say,
"I must get a photo with Santa today!"

CLICK!

CLICK!

CLICK!

Folks wanted snaps when he went to the gym,

CLICK!

And when he jumped in the pool for a swim.

CLICK!

When Santa tried yoga (he liked to keep healthy),
He even got asked for an upside-down selfie!

And after, when Santa was eating his lunch,
He was stopped for a photo between every munch!

"I must leave this liner!" sighed Santa. "I'm trapped!
I can't move a muscle without being snapped!"

CLICK!

The liner arrived at a port the next day.
Said Santa, "This looks like a nice place to stay!"

He crept to the gangway and chuckled with glee,
"I did it! Ho-Ho! No more photos for me!"

But then his heart sank as he heard a loud cheer . . .

"There he is!" cried the people.

"SANTA IS HERE!"

CLICK!

CLICK!

It looked like the whole of the city was there.

"Hey, Santa!" said Señor Gonzales, the mayor.

"We heard you were coming! And now, if you please,

Can we take a few photos? Santa, say cheese!"

"Oh bother!" thought Santa. "They know me here too!
I'll go somewhere far from this hullabaloo!"

But from Paris   to Sydney,

from Cairo   to Kyoto,

The folks cried, "It's Santa!" and asked for a photo.

He was snapped in Brazil on the Copacabana,

CLICK!

And stepping in zebra poop on the savannah.

CLICK!

The Great Wall of China drove Santa half mad,

At the old Taj Mahal things were nearly as bad.

When he reached the Grand Canyon, he thought, "Peace at last!
No one will find me. This place is so vast!"

He sat himself down for a doze in the shade,
Started to snore – and then sat up, dismayed.
Three busloads of children had seen Santa napping,
And stood with their cameras, all merrily snapping.

Santa saw one little boy on his own
And asked, "Do you mind if I borrow your phone?"

CLICK!

He thought to himself, "There's just one place I know
Where no one wants photos wherever I go!"

Behind a big cactus he made a quick call,
And heard something jingling in no time at all.

Down came the sleigh. Santa cried, "Phew!
Take me home, Little Elfie!" and –

WHOOSH! – off they flew.

"Thanks, Little Elfie, for coming so fast!"
He said, when they got to the North Pole at last.

North Pole

Rest of
the World

"It was really fun driving your sleigh," chuckled Elfie.
"And now, would you mind if I took a quick . . .

"SELFIE!"